Code White:

Frosted Wonderland

Taila Cantrell

Contents

Dedication

For all the bah-humbugs out there. I am one of you. Whether you are missing a loved one or some other struggle during the holiday season, you are seen.

Maybe a good fuck under a Christmas tree will fix everything.

Quote

One of the deepest secrets of life is that all that is really worth doing is what we do for others.

-Lewis Carroll

Chapter 1

December 12th, 2158

Snow was rare in Wonderland; I'd only seen it a handful of times, and certainly nothing like it was coming down now. My arms were laden down with bags as I rushed toward the Hummer. Hatter grinned at me from the driver's seat, clearly enjoying my suffering as I tried not to slip on the ice and snow covering the ground. Cheshire appeared out of nowhere, a bright purple hat pulled down over his ears. I pressed a kiss to his cheek as he opened the door for me, letting me climb into the front seat.

"Did you finally finish your shopping?" Hatter teased as I threw bags over the seat so I could get comfortable.

"I still need to get something for March and Mom," I muttered.

"I've never seen so many gifts." He said, grinning, "I thought our first Christmas together was a lot."

"Christmas was always important when I was a kid. Dad would make cookies, while Mom, Lily, and I decorated the tree. Mom was always home and engaged during December. Some of my best family memories are at Christmas time." I rambled as I warmed my hands in front of the heating vents. "Last year, we were too busy with all of the Red Party fallout to really celebrate. We need this after...." I trailed off, trying not to think of our failed wedding ceremony.

"I'm excited. I didn't mean to sound like I wasn't." Hatter said, laying a hand on my thigh.

"Yeah, plus watching Caterpillar have a stroke every time you bring home more bags is now my favorite pastime," Cheshire added in.

We all laughed as Hatter began slowly driving back home. We'd put out a call for some magick users with heating powers yesterday to try to melt some of the snow off the road, along with a large monetary award, they would receive free meals at the Grove while doing the work. It was the least we could offer since we had no other way to clear the roads aside from manpower. I waved at a man who was walking down the road, fire streaming from his hands. Even from a distance, I could tell he was far too skinny for his large frame. I hoped he enjoyed the free meals. I wish I could do more for the magick users in Wonderland. Obviously, we had worked hard over the last year to make a difference in their lives. It wasn't enough, not even close. They were appreciative of the bare minimum, and it made me sick. Magick users powered over half of Wonderland's survival with absolutely no recognition. I still couldn't wrap my mind around the fact that they were willing to continue their work after what the Red Queen had put them through.

"You're going to get a permanent wrinkle if you don't stop frowning," Cheshire said, interrupting my thoughts. "I mean, look at the one between Caterpillar's brow when we see him. You're far too pretty to have the same wrinkle as him."

"I'm telling him you said he looks old." Hatter laughed as he pulled the car in front of our building. He hopped out before Cheshire could respond, causing me to laugh as well when I turned to see the stricken look on his face.

"The boss man is already running me ragged in training," He whined as he slid out of the back seat. He opened my door for me, helping me down onto the snow-covered ground. He stole a kiss before dashing away to grab all of my bags. He was right, Caterpillar had been an absolute tyrant for two hours every night for three months. We all needed a break.

"I'll talk to him about it. I can't make any promises, but... It's Christmas time, we could use some time to relax." I admitted to Cheshire as we started to walk inside.

I couldn't help the smile that graced my face as we stepped into the warm building. Hatter and March had strung lights along all the doors and stairs. Lily had gone behind them and added a golden sparkly tinsel, creating a beautiful look in our home. We'd only officially been moved in for a month now. There had been months and months of renovations that had to be done for the building to be livable for everyone. We still had space for more people since Sammy, Patrick, and several others had refused our offer of their own apartment. We had four stories, two of which were completely dedicated to studio apartments. The other two had conference rooms, training space, and more. We had plenty of room to expand. It was truly our home; every time I stepped through the doors, it warmed my heart. I never could have thought anywhere but my childhood home would make me feel safe, but we had built an even better home. Everyone I loved had a space within these walls. It didn't hurt that it kept us all safer being together.

"Did you get your shopping done?" Caterpillar grumbled as we walked through the door.

"She said she still has to get something for March and Alcinda," Cheshire responded cheerfully.

"You don't need to go overboard, Alice. We all have everything that we need." Caterpillar chastised.

"That isn't what Christmas is about." I shot back as I made my way to the spare room, tucking my new bags alongside the rest. I might have gone a little overboard, but getting everyone something they would love and use was important to me.

"I scheduled a meeting tomorrow morning," Caterpillar said, standing in the doorway.

"About anything in particular?" I asked.

"We all need to be on guard. I got a call from Patrick. They've been seeing some stirrings around the boonies, one woman said she saw Jabberwocky." He explained.

I sucked in a breath, "It's been a couple of weeks since we've had a disturbance. You think they're gearing up for something big?"

"I do. With the bad weather, it would be a good time." Caterpillar said, pulling me against his chest as I approached him. "Just be careful if you go out again. I don't know what I'd do if something happened to you."

"Kill everyone?" I joked at the serious look on his face.

"If the Queen of Hearts hurts you, she won't get Wonderland. I'll burn the entire city down before she takes it." He growled into my ear as he picked me up.

"That might be a little extreme." I breathed out as he shut the door with his foot.

"I missed you." He ignored my comment, kissing my neck.

"I was only gone for a few hours," I argued.

"I don't see you enough, not with all the demands of being leaders of Wonderland. Why did we agree to do that again?" He asked after sitting me down. He bent down, unlacing and removing my boots. He ran his hands up both sides of my legs before unbuttoning my jeans. He yanked them down my legs so fast I yelped. He groaned when he found my bare pussy before him. I unzipped my jacket, tossing it behind me. I yanked my white t-shirt over my head as well, leaving me naked. "How did I get so lucky?"

"I need to be warmed up, Cater." I scooted closer to him, running my fingers through his hair.

I wasn't prepared for him to stand, gripping my hips to flip me over. "Are you already ready for me, princess?" He ran a hand down my back, gripping my ass before pressing a thick finger inside me. I moaned, pushing back. "Always so eager for me to take you." He removed his finger before lining himself up with my entrance. He moved slowly, torturing me. When he was finally fully seated, I pushed up on my arms, turning my head to look at him. "Creator, Alice. I love being inside you. Next time I have a meeting, I'm going to make you sit on my lap and warm my cock in front of everyone." I clenched my muscles at his words, causing him to groan again. He grabbed my hair, pulling my back to his chest. His hands roamed down, tweaking my nipples, brushing over my swollen clit. I moaned, grinding down on his cock as he played with me. "I'm never going to get enough of you."

"I certainly hope not," I said, reaching back to hold his head as he kissed my neck. Words weren't needed as we continued our game. The moment I'd get close, he'd pull away, pumping into me until I'd feel him shudder. Eventually, one of us would have to give in, and I knew it was going to be me, "Roman, please."

"What do you want, princess? Not trying to rush me, are you?" He chuckled in my ear as he pressed into me slowly, filling me up.

"Never." I gasped. He must have liked my answer because he started to move faster, matching his strokes with the fingers rubbing my clit. Before I could stop it, my orgasm crashed over me, sending me lurching forward. Caterpillar gripped my ass, slamming into me a few more times before spilling his seed inside me.

We lay on the bed together for a long time, my head resting on his chest. Eventually, I sat up, feeling the mess we made rushing down my legs, "Remind me I need to ask Mom about more of that tea she gave me last year. I'm almost out. The last thing we need is little Caterpillar's running around right now."

He was silent for a long moment, "Maybe someday."

I glanced back at him, seeing the emotions on his face, "We have our entire lives ahead of us. I would love to have your babies one day, but I want to have a few years of peace first."

He sighed, "I know. I'm just... I thought after the Red Queen we would settle down. Instead, we're running a city of twelve thousand people, about a third of which aren't sure we know what we're doing."

"You're doing the best you can, considering the circumstances. We all are." I pointed out, "It's going to be okay. I promise. We will get this Queen of Hearts stuff figured out soon. We've been close. At least we're in control of the city this time."

He pulled me into a hug, resting his head on my chest, "I love you."

"I love you more." I said, pressing my lips to his forehead, "But now I need a bath."

He chuckled, slapping my ass as I rushed out of the room. I entered our shared space, finding Cheshire on the bed, a book resting over his eyes. Quiet snores let me know he was asleep. I crept into the bathroom, a smile on my face. Even in these uncertain times, we all still felt loved and safe. That was all that mattered right now.

Chapter 2

❧ ❦

March

December 13, 2158

I was staring at the ceiling. The cracks in the plaster were far more interesting than the conversation happening around me. I still didn't understand why Caterpillar and Alice insisted I attend all the meetings. I wasn't involved in the political side of Wonderland. I could fight better now, but nothing like they could. My main purpose on a mission was to help out if anyone got hurt and Hatter or Alcinda weren't around. Stopping myself from groaning aloud was nearly impossible.

"March, how are the new business licenses working?" Rab asked, forcing my attention back to me.

"W-we've had some pushback, but Hatter has helped me with those few owners." I said, "I think g-giving more citizens an opportunity to build their own businesses is helping a lot. I've gotten several applications this week." I hadn't started sorting through them, since I'd only approved a few so far.

"If you need any help sorting through them, please let me know." He responded, a smile on his face. Rab had always been good to us, so his approval made me grin. When Hatter decided to join the Resistance, I had been hesitant. After everything I'd been through, I just wanted to live a quiet life. The idea of spending the rest of my life fighting still occasionally terrified me, but as my eyes rested on Alice I knew I'd made the right decision in following him.

She was wearing a sweater I made today, the red complimented her pale skin perfectly. I loved seeing her in something I made. I felt the same way as I glanced at the black beanie Hatter was wearing. I'd made it for him almost two years ago, but he still wore it regularly. I needed to buy more yarn so I could finish everyone's Christmas gifts. I had started crocheting when I was thirteen as a form of therapy. I loved how relaxing it was, and watching the people I loved wear things I made, made it even better.

"I think that covers everything for today," Caterpillar announced, "Please stay in pairs or groups when you're traveling, especially outside of the city. The Queen of Hearts is ramping up her attacks."

Everyone murmured their agreements, and stood to leave. I continued to sit, waiting until it was only Hatter, Caterpillar, Cheshire, and Alice in the room. "I'm going to st-steal Alice away for the rest of the day."

"We are supposed to head into training," Caterpillar argued.

"It's fine, Cater. March can train with me later," Alice interrupted, coming to my side and taking my arm, "We'll be back." She pulled me out of the room before he could respond.

The grin on her face had my heart racing with joy as we sprinted back to our apartment, "What the plan, Marchie?" She asked as she stuffed her wallet into her pants pocket.

"R-Rab's question about the business licenses reminded me that a new tea shop just opened. We're going to go check it out." I explained.

"Sounds like fun. Do you want to play in the snow when we get back?" She asked, joy alight in her eyes. The last couple weeks was the most relaxed I'd ever seen Alice, even before the Queen of Hearts had crashed our wedding.

"You think you can convince Caterpillar that is what we're doing for t-training?" I joked.

The mischievious grin she gave me as she yanked me out the door made my heart stop. I was so in love with this woman I'd do anything for her.

Valley's Tea Shoppe sat in a small building that would have been easy to miss if the line didn't wrap around the block. I hadn't considered a reservation when I'd decided to bring Alice here today. Thankfully, Alice didn't seem to mind the wait. Some people in line recognized us and chatted with her. Wonderland had accepted Alice without a second thought after her display of power. Most of the time she handled the responsibility with a grace that I admired, but I knew it weighed heavily on her shoulders.

"We're sorry for your wait. How many in your party?" A young woman asked as we approached the front of the line. Her eyes widened when she glanced to Alice, "Oh, Miss Young, I'm so sorry. If we'd realized you were coming we would have held a table for you."

"It's okay. Please treat me the way you would any other cusotmer." Alice waved her off, "We need a table for two."

"Absolutely, follow me this way," The woman said, fumbling with the menus.

The decor of the small shop was pretty, vines and plants hung from the ceiling, large comfy chairs and table were sat in perfect rows. The walls had been painted to look like the sky, making it feel like you were dining in a glass building. Most of the tables were full of people, chatting, and sipping piping hot tea from dainty cups.

"Here are your menus. We have the widest variety of teas that can be found in Wonderland. Our owner grows and cultivates them herself. We currently have a special tea available, the Frosted Wonderland, which does include alcohol. Your server will be with you shortly." The girl explained, before quickly making her exit.

"Well clearly I have to try the Frosted Wonderland." Alice said, "What are you going to have?"

Before I could respond a man slid up to our table with a large smile on his face, "Hello, Miss Young, I'll be your waiter today. My name is Trevor, have you picked out what you'd like to drink?" I didn't like the way he turned his body and attention toward Alice.

"I'd like the Frosted Wonderland." She said, as she reached across the table and grabbed my hand, "What do you want, hun?"

I grinned at her move, and responded, "I'll take the F-Frosted Wonderland as well." I gritted my teeth as I stuttered over the words. The smirk on Trevor's face was extremely familiar to me. I'd seen it on so many people in my life, even my own mother. They thought they were better than me, looked down on me for something as simple as how I spoke.

"Great, I'll get those in for you. Have you had a chance to look over the food menu. I highly recommend any of our egg sandwiches. They are amazing." He continued, still focused entirely on Alice. I saw his eyes drift down to her breasts several times, and an unfamiliar anger started to take root in my gut.

"Give us a few minutes to decide." Alice commanded, dismissing him. Once he had walked away, she sighed, "I don't like being a leader of the city. Everyone is either trying too hard to be on my good side or they hate me."

"You know you could step down," I pointed out. I had some hope she consider it. We could start truly building a life that wasn't centered around the drama of Wonderland.

"Maybe someday, March. I can't leave the people of Wonderland at the mercy of just anyone." She lowered her voice, "Not to even mention the Queen of Hearts."

I sighed. I knew that would be her answer. I fell in love with a woman of action. She couldn't leave behind all the people that still needed her, "I know, but don't forget that you deserve to have the life you want to."

"As long as I have you, Hatter, Caterpillar, and Cheshire I will be happy." She replied.

Before I could respond Trevor returned carrying two blue pots. He sat them both down. "Your tea, milady." He said, pouring Alice's tea first. "Just be careful, this drink is deceptively strong. We wouldn't want you to get drunk here."

Alice stiffened, "I'm sure I can handle it."

The look in his eye changed, "I have no doubt that you can handle quite a lot."

I grabbed my tea pot off the table, and poured my own cup, and said, "Thank you for bringing this. We need some more time to look at the menu."

He glanced at me for a moment, before nodding to Alice and walking off. "I should request a different server. I don't think I like what he was implying." Alice said, narrowing her eyes.

"It's okay, Ali. You know you're beautiful and powerful, people will flirt." I said, forcing myself to stay calm.

"That may be true, but it's unprofessional." She argued.

I smiled, "What did you get everyone for Christmas?" I asked changing the subject.

"I got Caterpillar a new pair of boots and a little kit of stuff for him to use on his bike." Alice started, lighting up with joy as she went over everything she'd gotten for our little family. I basked in her joy as she spoke. Alice warmed parts of me I didn't know were cold. I had been in love with Hatter since I was fourteen, but my love for Alice was different. If I loved Hatter the way I loved water, I loved Alice like she was the sun. They were both necessary for my survival, but I needed them differently. Loved them differently.

I finally took a sip of the tea that had cooled down. As soon as it hit my tongue I groaned, "This is too good."

Alice laughed as she lifted her own cup to her lips. I watched as her throat moved with the swallow. I couldn't help but imagine her swallowing all of me instead. "Oh, he was right this is a dangerous drink. We're going to walk out of here drunk."

I snorted, "I t-think we can handle it."

Trevor approached our table again, "Are you ready to order?"

"I'll take the Kraken's plate and she'll b-be having the Wonder special." I responded, pulling his attention away from Alice.

"Will that be all?" He asked, looking me up and down with a strange look.

"Yes, and please don't disturb us again until you bring our food." I commanded, handing him our menus. I was trying to channel Caterpillar and Hatter's confidence, but the sneer on his face as he stormed away told me it didn't work.

I settled back into my seat, looking at Alice. She smiled and said, "You handled that well."

"Thank you." I responded with a relieved sigh. I didn't like being rude to anyone, but that man needed to leave my woman alone.

We sat and talked for a long time, the patrons in the shop slowly dwindling down until our section was completely empty. Alice looked around and said, "Do you think it usually takes this long to get our food?"

"I'll go try to find someone." I offered.

Just as I stood, Trevor appeared carrying our food. "Sorry about that wait. I just wanted to be sure y'all didn't feel disturbed." I clenched my jaw at the snark, but said nothing as he sat our food before us. "I'll be back with the check later." He said before walking away.

The food looked amazing. My plate held a small piece of fish surrounded by various colorful sides. Alice's was filled with an array of tiny sandwiches. I only recognized a few of the cheeses and vegetables that graced them, but it look good nonetheless. It was all served on plates that perfectly matched our tea cups. "You have a good eye for business, March." Alice complimented, "Do you like what Caterpillar assigned you to do?"

I thought for a moment, "Mostly. It doesn't feel like it's as impactful as what everyone else does."

"I disagree. I think giving the citizens of Wonderland more opportunities to grow and thrive is far more impactful than anything I do." She argued.

I hadn't considered that. She was right. The citizens of Wonderland were the reason we did everything we'd done. If they had more chances to live normal lives then we were doing our job. "I hadn't c-considered that. Thank you."

Alice reached across the table and grabbed my hand, "I know there's a lot of things you don't share with the rest of us. I hope that you know we're here for you. I love you so much, Maxton. You being part of my life is a blessing."

Tears pricked my eyes, and I squeezed her hand back, "I-I love you, Ali. Thank you for picking me."

We ate in silence, quiet groans of appreciation leaving us. Once I had finished my entire plate and drained every last drop of my tea pot I stood, "I'm going to run to the restroom. Are you okay?"

"I'll be fine, but you may have to roll me out of here." She joked, patting her completely flat stomach.

I wasn't in the bathroom long, but when I returned Trevor was looming over Alice. I could tell from a distance he had a grip on her shoulder. I couldn't see her hands, but just seeing the way he manhandled her set me off. I glanced down at the table next to me and noticed the smallest fork I'd ever seen. Before I could think twice I grabbed it, striding across the room and plunging the tines into the hand that touched Alice. Trevor drew back, screaming as the fork was imbedded into his hand, "N-never touch a woman without permission again." I spat, yanking Alice up from her seat.

She grabbed her wallet, throwing a stack of bills on the table before I pulled her out of the restaurant.

My heart beat fast as we ran to the Hummer, emotions tangled in my chest as panic clawed up my throat. My hands were shaking, but I never let go of Alice. Just as we approached the Hummer, Alice pulled ahead of me. She swung open the back door, pushing me inside. Once I was seated, she pushed my head between my legs and rubbed my back, "It's okay. You're fine. Just take some deep breaths." I let Alice's calming voice wash over me, forced the swirling feeling back into the depths of my mind. When I sat up, Alice climbed into my lap, pressing her full lips to mine, "That was kind of hot."

"The panic attack?" I joked.

"The jealousy. That's not usually my thing, but the way you just stabbed him for touching me. I didn't even have a chance to zap him." She ran her hands down my chest.

As I continued to calm down and start to feel normal I asked, "How do you handle my outbursts so well? Mo-most people can't deal with someone having a panic attack."

Alice leaned her head back against the seat, moving her body slightly bringing my awareness to the way that her core pressed against me. I felt blood rush to my dick, making it harder to focus as she answered, "When my mom died, or at least when I thought she died, I didn't handle it well. My teen years were rife with random panic attacks. I couldn't hardly walk down a sidewalk in the city without the fear I'd die just like I'd seen her die. Dad and Lily helped a lot. Eventually I stopped letting the fear hold me back."

Fear had been the only thing I'd known most of my life. Anger was still new to me, and I liked the way the rage felt. I felt powerful as I stabbed Trevor. The fact I'd crashed after the fact sucked. "I'm sorry you went through that." I finally said.

"It's nothing like what you've been through." She said, leaning forward as she wrapped her hands around my neck.

The movement had her brushing over my erection, I choked out, "Alice."

"What Marchie?" She asked, a mischievous look in her eyes.

"We're in the c-car." I pointed out.

"Exactly, no one will see us." She shot back. Before I could stop her, she shimmed into the floorboard between my legs. "May I have a taste?"

"Of course." I groaned. Without a hesitation she undid my pants, pulling my weeping cock out. I dug my nails into the leather seats, forcing myself not to cum just from the look in her eyes.

"I love your cock. It's curved so perfectly. Every time you fuck me you hit just the right spots." Her dirty words had me moaning, "Will you cum down my throat, Maxton?"

"Uh huhhhh." Was the only response I could come up with. Her mouth devoured me, as she pressed herself all the way down my cock. When I hit the back of her throat my back bowed, causing her to gag around me. The feeling was unlike anything I'd felt before. I gripped her hair, forcing her to hold the position as I fucked her mouth. "L-look at me."

Her blue eyes lifted to mine, and the love inside them was all I needed to spill my seed down her throat. She drank it greedily, her lips popping as she pulled away.

"L-let me help you." I said, reaching for her.

"Not this time, honey. I just wanted to make you feel good." Alice said, climbing into the front seat after pressing a kiss to my lips.

"I don't think I'll ever get enough of you." I admitted after I fixed my clothes and crawled to the front.

"I know I'll never get enough of you." She pressed a kiss to my cheek before she pulled out of our spot and headed home.

Anywhere Alice was would be my home.

Chapter 3

✦✦✦✦✦ ✦✦✦✦✦

Hatter

December 18th, 2158

Alice was sick. She'd barely been out of bed for the last two days. I was convinced that she picked something up when she and March went out. I carried a bowl of hot soup to her right now. She hadn't had a bite to eat in well over twenty-four hours, and Caterpillar was about to insist on something crazy if she didn't eat something soon.

"Hey, Ali," I said as I entered the dark room. The only way you could even tell she was in here was the lump of blankets in the middle of the bed and the tissues surrounding her, "I've brought you some soup, baby. I need you to eat something." The gray lump moved slightly, but didn't respond. I set the bowl on the bedside table and sat next to her. "Caterpillar is out there losing his shit. If you don't get some food down soon, he's half likely to make your mother heal you. The snow is still coming down, so as soon as you get feeling better, we can go outside and play in it."

"Her healing doesn't work on things like this." The lump grumbled.

I furrowed my eyebrows, "Why?"

"How the hell should I know?" Alice snapped, sitting up. Her hair was tied up in a messy bun, and the neck of the t-shirt she wore was wet. Somehow, even sick and gross, I still found her beautiful. "It just doesn't."

"Well, I thought magick could do anything," I said. "Since you're sitting up, why don't you take a few sips of this?" I shoved the bowl into her hands.

She glared at me, but put her lips to the bowl and tilted it back. Within minutes, she had drained it completely and handed it back to me. "Can I go back to sleep now?" Alice grumbled.

"You may. Caterpillar shouldn't bust the door down now." I joked, pressing my lips to her head.

I closed the door behind me as I exited the room. I nearly ran into Caterpillar as he came storming up the hallway. "Whoa, whoa. She ate. Let her rest."

"She needs to be healed." He growled.

"She said, healing magick won't help this cold she has." I explained, "I think we should just let her sleep it off."

"Well, what's the point of healing magick then?" Caterpillar said, throwing his hands in the air. "I don't like this. It's the perfect time for the Queen of Hearts to attack her."

"She'll never get into our home," Cheshire said, appearing out of nowhere. "I just put in a system that will alert us if anyone approaches who doesn't live here."

I didn't understand tech the way that Cheshire did, so I couldn't imagine how anything like that could exist. Caterpillar stared at him for a moment before deflating. "I guess I'll go see if the magick users have managed to clear the roads."

"This snow isn't going to stop coming down anytime soon. Why not just give them a break?" I asked.

"It means the city is vulnerable." He said before striding away.

Cheshire and I looked at each other before I shrugged. "At least he's doing something other than worrying about her."

"I was actually coming to talk to you. Follow me." Cheshire directed before he darted off to his lair. The room was dark due to the curtains covering the windows, but I knew better than to turn a light on in here. Cheshire liked his room a certain way, and I wasn't going to disturb it. "I found this on one of the cameras I installed over at the Grove. Tell me what you see."

I squinted at the screen as he turned it my way, "That looks like the Queen of Hearts." The video was grainy and hard to see, but the bright red curls were hard to miss. "Why would she be there?"

"I don't know, but I don't like it at all." Cheshire said, "You are the one with the connections around town. Do you think you could talk to some people, see if anyone saw her inside?"

"I'll see what I can do. Will you keep an eye on the sickie for me?" I asked. I didn't want to leave Alice alone while she was feeling sick, but I knew what Cheshire was asking me to do was important. Months had passed since the Queen revealed herself, and we were no closer to knowing anything about her than we were when she showed up. It was infuriating. The woman didn't just come into existence to ruin our wedding.

"Thanks, man. Let me know if you find anything out." Cheshire said, turning back to his screens. I watched him for a moment as he began typing, the screen scrolling faster than I could keep up with.

I left the room, sneaking into the bathroom and taking the quietest shower I'd ever taken. When I left the bathroom, Alice was sitting up, staring at the bedroom door. "I need some water." She croaked.

I rushed from the room, making her a glass of water as quickly as humanly possible. "Here ya go, sweetheart. I was just about to go out. Is there anything else you need right now?"

Her bright red nose scrunched up, "A shower would be nice, but I think I can handle that on my own."

"Cheshire is in his room. Do you want me to have him come sit with you?" I asked.

She shook her head and crawled out of bed. I could tell the movement made her feel exhausted, but she stood before me, "I know I stink, but can I have a hug?"

I grinned, pulling her body against mine, "You never have to ask. I don't care how sick or dirty you might be. Hugging you is my favorite thing to do."

She gave a small laugh before dissolving into a coughing fit. I grabbed her water and handed it to her. After several minutes, she sat on the end of the bed. "I hate being sick."

"I know. At least it doesn't happen very often." I responded. Alice had been ill for months after taking the Red Queen's power. She had slept so much that I don't know how we managed to function. I never wanted to see her use that power again. It was like it had burned her from the inside out. The Red Queen's final act of pain had tortured Alice for months. At least this was just a cold; she'd feel better in a few days.

"Weren't you going somewhere?" Alice asked, drawing me from my thoughts.

"Oh... yeah. Cheshire..." I stopped, realizing I didn't want her to be stressed about this while she was trying to feel better. "Cheshire just needs me to run an errand for him. I shouldn't be gone that long."

She narrowed her eyes, but ultimately nodded, "Okay. Be careful."

"You know it," I said, pressing a kiss to her head again before I left.

The Grove was quiet today. I wasn't surprised considering the weather. In fact, I was more surprised that they were open at all. The snow was bad enough that I had to walk here. I didn't feel like digging the Hummer out from under the two feet of snow that had accumulated on it.

"How can we help you today, sir?" The host asked, recognizing me immediately. I hated that, before Alice and Caterpillar took over running Wonderland, I could operate anonymously most of the time. Now I was lucky if people didn't ask me to pass messages along for them.

"I need to take a look at the receipts for the last three nights," I said, casually.

"I'm sorry, but I can't let you have access to guest information like that." He argued.

"I can contact Roman Ainsworth to come down here if need be," I said. I didn't like having to use my connection to Caterpillar to force things, but I knew the moment his eyes widened that I had won.

"No need. Right this way." He said, leading me through the restaurant and kitchen to a small room in the back. "Everything we have will be right here." I only keep these for about a week before we toss them out."

"Thanks," I said, taking a seat in the leather chair behind the desk. He stood there for a moment staring at me, before finally turning on his heel and leaving. I needed to get his name before I left. I didn't like his attitude at all.

The small pieces of paper before me were barely big enough to read. The stack was huge, too. I had no idea the Grove was doing this much business.

Hours later, I was still sorting through tiny pieces of paper. Nothing I'd found gave any indication that the Queen of Hearts had been here. I was about to give up when I noticed a receipt with a familiar name. "That motherfucker." Dodo's name, Gavin Danara, was written on a check that clearly was for several people. Dodo would absolutely collude with the Queen of Hearts against us, but I forced myself to finish going through the rest of the stack. No other names, familiar or unfamiliar, stood out except for his. We'd been trying to figure out a way to shut his business down for months. Maybe I finally had enough proof of his collusion that I could make it happen. We needed to stake out his business.

I picked up my phone, dialing Cheshire. "' Ello?" His voice was groggy.

"How is Alice?" I asked as I found the back exit of the Grove.

"She's asleep again. She ate another bowl of soup and showered." He said, "Did you find anything?"

"Dodo was here the night she was seen." I said, before rushing to add, "It was a big bill, so I think it's very likely he met with her. I'm going to call Patrick and see if he can get some eyes on his store."

"We need more proof than that to arrest him." Cheshire groaned.

"I know," I responded. "Keeping a closer eye on him is all we can do for now."

"Who do you think she really is?" He asked.

I hummed for a moment, contemplating the question, "I don't know. Duchess thinks she's related to her father. Which makes sense if she grew up calling her aunt. I don't see any relation, though. Frederick doesn't look anything like the Queen of Hearts." I knew I was rambling, but I hated feeling like I didn't have any answers, "Who knows. Does it really matter?"

"I guess not. But if we knew her true identity, maybe I could find out more about her." He responded, "We'll talk more when you get back."

I hung up and began the trek back through the snow to our apartment. Three months had passed since the Queen of Hearts stopped our wedding. I hated that we hadn't immediately finished the ceremony. Alice should be my wife; she was my wife in every way that truly mattered. We all felt the same way, and yet our marriage had been placed on the back burner so that we could handle the Queen of Hearts. Wonderland did need us, I knew that better than anyone. I wanted to do what I could for Wonderland. I lived here, the people I loved lived here. As far as anyone knew, it's the last standing structure on earth. We may very well be the last humans. The least we could do is keep our city safe. The line of thinking had me clinching my fists. I'd lost my father to the stupid hope that Wonderland wasn't the last city. He'd never been seen again. Ten years had passed, and there were still moments I expected him to walk through the door in his brown suit, ready for work.

Snow started to fall heavily, making the trek back to our home even longer than usual. I managed to keep my feet for the most part, but when our building came into view, I breathed a sigh of relief. I took the stairs two at a time, more than ready to climb into my warm bed. As I opened the door, I found Alice and Caterpillar standing in the living room.

"You should be in bed." I pointed out.

Alice turned toward me with a huff, "I'm feeling better. He's making it impossible for me to do anything."

"She wants to work." Caterpillar growled, "She's barely moved for days, and now she's up trying to go to stupid meetings."

"A meeting with Sammy and Patrick isn't stupid!" Alice stomped her foot as she spoke.

I forced myself to hold in a laugh, "Why don't we just have them come here? I need to talk to Patrick anyway. Alice can get comfy on the sofa, and we can just talk."

"I don't like it," Caterpillar said, crossing his arms. "She needs to rest more."

"Alice will go back to bed as soon as they leave." I offered, sending her a look when she started to argue.

Caterpillar glanced at her, and she sighed, "I will even eat solid food."

He smiled and pulled her into his arms, "Thank you, princess."

It was a whirlwind as I rushed into the kitchen, staring into our fridge. I decided to make Alice a simple chicken dish with some veggies on the side. It wasn't fancy, but it would be filling for her. I heard a knock on the front door, but I didn't stop what I was doing. The voices floated in as I finished plating Alice's dinner.

"Sorry, guys. Ali has been sick for days, she's going to eat while we talk." I announced as I entered the room.

Sammy and Patrick had taken chairs right next to each other. It was easy to see the family resemblance when they sat next to each other. The same brown hair and warm brown eyes, the arch of their nose and point of their chin were the same as well.

"Miss Alice, is there something we can do for you? We could have postponed this meeting." Sammy said, fatherly love in his voice.

"I'm fine, Sam. I need to do something other than lie in bed." She smiled at me as I handed her the plate of food, "What has been going on in the boonies?"

"It's been mostly quiet. We've caught a couple of weapon shipments heading through, but both times the drivers were completely unaware what they were carrying." He explained.

"They are smart, that's for sure." I said, "But I think I know who is up to it all. Is Cheshire going to join us?"

"I'm right here," Cheshire responded from behind me, causing me to jump.

"I hate it when you do that." I growled at him, "Today, Cheshire found some grainy video footage of the Queen of Hearts exiting the Grove. I went over there today and shuffled through their receipts. Take a wild guess whose name I found."

Caterpillar spoke first, "Dodo."

"Correct. I think that Dodo is helping the Queen of Hearts and what remains of the Red Party." I said.

"But why?" Alice asked, her food abandoned next to her, "We have left him alone to operate in peace."

"Money, of course," Sammy responded.

He was right, but that didn't mean I was happy about it. "I want eyes on him and his store twenty-four seven until we catch him with something so that we can shut him down."

"I agree." Caterpillar added, "And get us pictures if possible. I don't want him to be able to garner sympathy with any of the citizens."

Alice nodded, "I don't like this at all. Money isn't everything. What else could Dodo gain from helping her?"

The room was silent as we all contemplated her question. I couldn't think of a good reason for him to help her that wasn't about money.

"Does it matter?" Cheshire asked, "We finally have a good reason to look into what he does."

"Exactly," Caterpillar said, standing from his place next to Alice, "Is there anything else we need to discuss tonight? I'd like Alice to finish eating and head back to bed."

She narrowed her eyes at him, but I could see the exhaustion in her face. "I don't have anything else right now. I think we meet up after Christmas, unless something happens before then." I said.

Everyone agreed. Sammy and Patrick said their goodbyes quickly and left. Alice was yawning when I turned back to her. "It's okay if you need to go lie down." The dark circles under her eyes stood out more than they had just a couple of hours before.

"Thank y'all for taking care of me." She said, pressing a kiss to my cheek, then Caterpillar's, and finally Cheshire's. She trudged back down the hallway, leaving us all standing in silence for several minutes.

I realized suddenly I hadn't seen March all day. Once Alice was out of the room, I turned toward Caterpillar, "Where's March?"

"He's taking care of something for me." He responded cryptically.

"Do I want to know?" I asked.

"I'm not going to tell you even if you do," Caterpillar said, before leaving the room.

I looked at Cheshire, who shrugged, yawned, and said, "I'm going back to bed."

With that, I was standing alone in our living room. It wasn't often that I found myself with nothing to do and no one around. The weather was too bad to go for a run or a drive, so I sat down on the couch. The moment my head was resting comfortably, I was drifting off to sleep.

Chapter 4

Alice

December 20th, 2158

"It's only five days until Christmas! You can't keep me in this house any longer!" I shouted as I skirted around Caterpillar, rushing toward the door. I'd been feeling better for two days, but he was having none of it.

"You don't need to be out in this weather! You could get sick again." He said, stomping after me.

"I'm not that fragile, Roman. I'll be fine." I said, turning around to take him in. He had pulled on his leather jacket that hugged the muscles in his arms and chest. My mouth went dry with want, but I shook it away. "Are you going with me to get decorations for the tree?"

"We haven't even gotten a tree." He pointed out.

"Don't remind me. We're so far behind." I groaned. I hated being sick; I didn't have the time to lose, especially not at this time of year. I still needed to finish shopping for Mom and March.

Caterpillar sighed, "Fine, but I want you to check in with me at least every two hours."

"I'm not a child," I argued.

"No, you're much more important to me than some random child. Every two hours. Understood, princess?"

I nodded, "Love you."

He kissed me soundly before escorting me out of the building. The snow was still falling, though less heavily than it had been before. I wanted to spend time playing in it, but I had to get the decorations purchased and delivered before I did anything else today.

• • • ● ● • ● ● • • •

I was lucky that any of the shops were open today, but I managed to get everything I needed. Plus, I found the perfect gift for my mother. I was walking back home, enjoying the feel of the cold wind on my face, when someone called out my name.

"Alice. Miss Alice!" The panting man skidded to a stop just in front of me, "I need your help. Can you come with me?"

"What's wrong?" I asked, glancing at the bags hanging from my arms.

"Some magick users are fighting two streets over. I tried to break it up, and one of them burned me." He rolled up his sleeve, showing a very fresh burn.

"Go to my building, drop these bags off, and ask my mother to heal that," I commanded, handing him my bags, before I ran in the direction he'd pointed.

It didn't take me long before I heard the commotion of a fight. I found the crowd after about fifteen minutes of running. Now I understood why that man had been out of breath. I pushed my way through the crowd, coming to a stop to stare at the two men circling one another. The ground around them was devoid of snow, and I gasped when fire flickered along one of their fists.

"Hey, break it up," I shouted, striding toward them. Before I could get to them, a blaze of fire rushed toward me. I dove out of the way, tweaking my shoulder as I hit the ground. I growled, calling my magick to my hands before realizing electricity wasn't going to make this situation any better. I took a deep breath, calling my power-sapping ability to the front. I hadn't used it since I took all of Penthea's power. It wasn't worth the risk considering how long it had taken me to recover from that day. I watched them for a moment, deciding the best way to handle this situation. When they went for each other again, I jumped in between them. Heat licked all around me, but I cast my power out, smothering the magick.

Both of the men stumbled back, cursing. "Maybe that'll teach you to act better in my city," I growled. Their powers twisted in my chest, fighting to be let out or absorbed into my own magick. I took a deep breath, "Why the hell are you fighting?"

One of the men moved closer to me, his brown hair dripping sweat, "Saul claimed that he would get the roads clear by himself so he could have all of the prize money."

I cut my eyes toward the other man, Saul, who at least knew to look ashamed. "Anyone who contributes to keeping the roads of the city clear will receive the same amount of money and food. You both should know better than to act this way in front of normal citizens. What kind of a name are you giving the magick users of Wonderland?"

"I'm sorry." The man said, "I'm Garrett. It's nice to meet you, Miss Young."

I took a deep breath, realizing both of these men had suffered enough. I took Garrett's offered hand, feeding his magick back to him. "I wish it had been under better circumstances."

Saul approached and growled, "Give it back."

I scowled, "Maybe if you ask nicer." I lowered my voice, moving into his personal space, "You aren't going to intimidate me. I could eat you for breakfast. I don't want your magick, but you chose to make a scene here today. This is the consequence."

He stared at me for a long moment before finally gritting out, "I apologize for my actions today."

"Better," I muttered, taking his hand and slowly feeding his magick back to him. His shoulders relaxed once I'd given everything back.

"Thank you," He nodded, before turning to walk away.

I watched the men both go in opposite directions before I turned to the crowd, "Please be careful heading to your homes." I said. The crowd slowly dissipated, leaving me standing in the center of the street alone. I glanced toward the grey sky, as snow fell onto my face, I closed my eyes. My body shook slightly from the use of my ability. I hadn't used it enough to be used to the after effects. I still didn't know how I'd managed to do what I'd done to Penthea and stayed standing in the hours afterward. This wasn't nearly as serious, but I could feel my magick pulsing in my chest.

"Al! Are you okay?" I turned to see Cheshire running toward me, "I've been looking for you for twenty minutes. That guy scared all of us to death." Before I could respond, my knees buckled. Thankfully, Cheshire managed to catch me before I fell into the snow. "What's wrong?"

"I held their powers for too long." I said, "I just need to go home and lie down for a bit."

"You shouldn't have come here alone." He grunted as he adjusted my body in his arms.

"I can't let magick users run wild in Wonderland. The regular citizens are still adjusting to the idea of magick. It's my responsibility to handle any issues the magick users have." I argued as he began the trek home.

"Everything isn't on your shoulders, Al. I know it may feel that way, especially when it comes to magick, but with stuff like this, you need to ask for help." Cheshire said, "We're your partners. It's our job to shoulder some of your burdens."

I contemplated his words for a long while. In a way, he was right, but Caterpillar didn't have magick. Cheshire and March both had strange feelings about their magick, and Hatter was banned from using his since his hair turned whiter every time he did. Magick was my entire world; it always had been. I felt responsible for all of the magick users that lived in Wonderland. They were a small minority of the population, but they deserved to be treated in the same way as everyone else. Especially after everything they'd been put through by the Red Party. Finally, I said, "I know you're right, Ches, but you have to admit... I'm more invested in them than all of you are."

His dark blue eyes held an emotion I didn't understand as he responded, "I know I haven't been as excited about magick as I could have been. Honestly, not knowing which of my parents my abilities come from bothers me. It's just another thing they never had a chance to tell me or teach me."

"Oh, baby. I'm so sorry." I said, pressing my lips to his cheek. "Take your time. Your magick will be there when you're ready to learn more about it."

"In the meantime, I need you to promise me that you'll come to at least one of us about this stuff." He insisted.

"I will do my best," I responded. I couldn't give him a false promise. If I felt like I needed to do something, I didn't always stop to discuss it with someone else. It would take time for me to learn how to reach out in that way.

"That's all any of us can ask." Cheshire said, "Now, why don't you rest. When you get back up, we can finally decorate the tree."

I hadn't even noticed that we'd finally arrived at home, but I didn't complain as Cheshire carried me to our bed and laid me down.

I woke up feeling much better; my magick rested easily as I showered and dressed. I decided to slip into a set of fuzzy white pajamas I'd bought recently. Once I was dressed, I made my way out into the living room. Only for tears to well up in my eyes. All four guys were standing throughout the room. A huge tree took up one entire wall, and everything I'd bought to decorate with was laid out waiting for me.

"Good to see you, sleepyhead. Ready to decorate the t-tree?" March asked as he handed me a cup of steaming liquid. I held it for a moment, letting its warmth absorb into my body. I took a sip, and a lemony taste burst across my tongue unexpectedly.

"This is good." I said, shocked, "Where did you get it?"

"From Vallie's Tea Shoppe. I went back over there to a-apologize to them for the... incident." March said, a blush working its way over his cheeks. "The owner told me that Trevor quit. She wasn't even aware of what had happened. I-I explained what happened. She gave me some tea samples and told me to come back soon."

My eyebrows hit my hairline. I glanced toward Hatter, but lowered my voice, "You didn't... You know?"

March furrowed his eyebrows for a moment, and I wiggled my fingers at him. His eyes widened, and he rushed to say, "N-no, no of c-course not."

I laid my hand on his shoulder, "It's okay if you did. It's just odd that she was so kind about you stabbing her server."

"He harassed you." March pointed out, "I d-don't use my magick like that."

"You could," I said, casually. It wouldn't bother me if he did. At least it would mean he felt comfortable with what he could do.

"Come on, woman. Let's get to decorating." Cheshire said, ending the awkward silence that had started to hang in the air.

I clapped my hands together and grabbed some silver tinsel that was lying on the couch. It was what I chose to present myself, purple and pink bulbs would represent Cheshire. I'd found some dark red ribbon to wrap around the tree that reminded me of Caterpillar's favorite shirt. March had actually chosen the lights that were already strung around the tree, a light sparkling green that almost looked like they'd grown from the branches.

After all the decorations were on the tree, I stood admiring our hard work. Hatter stood next to it, hanging a few bulbs up high while Caterpillar climbed onto his chair to place the golden star I'd purchased on the top. "Wait. I have a better idea." I said suddenly, rushing toward them. I plucked the white beanie Hatter wore off his head and handed it to Caterpillar, "Put this on top instead. Then it'll have something for each of us."

Hatter laughed and pulled me into his arms. "I love you."

"I love you. All of you. Thank you for taking care of me. I know it isn't always easy." I said, eyes filling with tears. The four of them could make me forget about any problem we faced if we were together.

We all stood there, taking in the tree for a long moment before Hatter's hand roamed over my breast. "I have an idea." He said, the growl in his voice sending shivers down my spine. In one move, he yanked my pjs down, exposing my body to the room. "March, hand me that extra string of lights."

"I like where your mind is at," Caterpillar growled as he pulled my top off. My nipples pebbled under the cool air of the room.

Hatter approached, "On your knees, facing the tree." I followed his directions without hesitation, my heartbeat pulsing in my clit. I closed my eyes as hands roamed over my body, driving me higher toward pleasure. I knew I couldn't cum without stimulation, but I was close. "Hands behind your back." He instructed. I felt warmth and plastic as he began to tie what I could only assume were lights around my body. A pinch to my nipple as he tied the rope around my chest had me spreading my legs wider. The feeling of the warm rope pressing between my legs was almost more than I could bear. Once I was fully tied, Hatter pressed a hand between my shoulder blades, pushing me forward. I realized what I must look like, naked, tied up with Christmas lights, my pussy on display and dripping for my men underneath our tree. "I'm going to take you first, then Caterpillar, then Cheshire, and finally March. We are going to fill you with so much cum that you'll still be dripping Christmas morning." Hatter growled before he slammed inside of me. I screamed out, blinded by pleasure as he pounded into me relentlessly. Time didn't exist as he took my body. When I felt his seed fill me, I groaned, my own orgasm just at the edge of my awareness. The hands on my hips changed, and I knew when Caterpillar began to press his larger cock into me.

"You're my pretty little princess, aren't you?" He asked.

"Yes, sir." I moaned, pressing back into him.

A sharp slap to my ass was his response, "You're only going to get what I'm willing to give you." Caterpillar fucked me for what felt like hours, his cock bringing tears to my eyes as he pressed into the most sensitive parts of my pussy. The pleasure was almost too much, but still I couldn't cum. When he groaned and several pulses of warm seed spilled into me again, I cried out.

My pussy ached from the abuse, but I knew they weren't done. I knew when soft hands caressed my back that it was Cheshire's turn. His fingers pressed into my pussy, "You're dripping with their cum, Ali. I think mine needs to be in the mix."

"Please, Ches." I moaned, words were almost impossible as he brushed over my clit.

He laughed before plunging inside of me. Thankfully, Cheshire took me quickly, clearly excited by the show the others had put on before him. Before he finished, he peppered my ass with slaps, causing heat to build. I could feel the combined juices of them rolling down my thighs as he pulled out.

There was a moment of emptiness before I felt March sink to his knees behind me. "I want you to cum first, Ali."

I nearly sobbed in relief as March's deft fingers moved to my clit, rubbing circles in the exact pace that I liked. "Cum for m-me, beautiful girl."

His words were all the permission I needed to come undone. I screamed as my orgasm washed over me, my walls pulsing around nothing. Before the pleasure subsided, I felt March enter me. His strokes were not hurried; he took every twitch and groan in stride as he fucked me. Finally, just before he came, he pulled out, and I felt his cum paint my pussy and ass. Fingers followed soon, scooping the cum up and pressing it inside me.

Hands lifted me, untying the ropes and saying soothing words as I was carried to our room. A warm cloth carefully wiped away all of the mess that dripped from between my legs. All four men surrounded me in bed as I drifted into a dreamless sleep, completely satisfied.

Chapter 5

December 21th, 2158

"Why are we celebrating with the family now?" Cheshire asked, as we finished wrapping the last of the gifts we'd bought for the people we loved. We had already agreed that we weren't going to exchange gifts with each other until Christmas morning.

"Because we're all assigned to at least one day of patrolling the city or handing out food every day except tonight." I pointed out. Everyone agreed that we needed to make sure everyone in Wonderland was warm and fed, considering how bad the weather had been. Hatter was going to be driving out into the suburbs and boonies to make sure everyone still had power. If need be, we would find somewhere in the city to house everyone.

"Don't remind me," Caterpillar growled, "I didn't want to have to do any of this, but everyone is in more danger with this weather. The Queen of Hearts could use this as a way to attack the city while we're weak."

I put a hand on his shoulder, "It's okay, bossman. We're going to have Christmas morning together."

"Why don't y'all get ready? We've already showered." Hatter chimed in from the hallway. His hair was still dripping water from his shower, but he was already dressed in a dark green silk shirt and black pants that hugged his body sinfully.

I grabbed Caterpillar before he could object, and dragged him toward the master bathroom. Once we entered the bedroom, I started peeling my clothes off. Caterpillar did the same, his longer legs eating up the distance between us before I could reach the shower. I squealed as he picked me up, throwing me over his shoulder as he bent to turn the water on. Once it was to his liking, he sat me down, climbing in behind me. We showered together, washing each other slowly. We didn't speak as we exited the shower. Caterpillar dried me off as I fumbled through a drawer looking for my makeup. I carefully applied some black kohl under my eyes before swiping a light pink over my lips. When I turned around, Caterpillar was dressed, "I picked a dress out for you."

I followed him into the bedroom, where he held up a knee-length, emerald green dress. "It's perfect."

I dressed quickly, before I ended up staring into the closet at my shoe options. Caterpillar sat on the bed, watching me, "You could be more helpful."

"Oh, I've got to pick out the dress and the shoes." He laughed, "Get the silver ones."

I bent down, pulling them onto my foot, before realizing I couldn't easily lace them up. Once they were on my feet, I walked over to Caterpillar. He wasn't prepared for me to kick my leg up, pressing my shoe into his chest. The look he gave me made me want to peel my clothes off and straddle him, but I waited as he carefully tied the straps of my shoe around my ankle. Before I could lift my other leg, he grabbed my knee, putting my other foot onto his thigh. "You're lucky we have to be at dinner in ten minutes, or I'd turn you over my lap for that little move."

I grinned, "Oh yeah? I'm sure ten minutes is enough for something."

He ran his hands up my legs, stopping on the back of my thighs. "You know I like to take my time with you."

"Y'all about ready?" Hatter shouted from somewhere in the apartment.

"It's time to go, princess," Caterpillar said, standing up. I groaned, but followed him out of the bedroom. Christmas was one of the few times of the year that everyone made an effort to spend time with one another and set aside our responsibilities. Tonight was about family.

We had rented the top floor of the Grove to celebrate together. Mom, Rab, and Lewis had beaten us here. Lewis toddled up to me the moment we stepped inside. I swept him up into my arms, pressing my nose into his light brown curls, "Hey Lewie, are you excited to open presents?"

"Yeah." He said, bouncing in my arms until I was forced to sit him down so he could run up to March. March swept him into his arms, and they proceeded to have an extremely hard-to-understand conversation. We had decided to celebrate Lewis' birthday in September since we were unsure of his exact age and date of birth. We were fairly certain he was around four now. He wasn't a particularly talkative child, but he was curious and always into something. March and Lewis shared a sense of purity that I'd never seen in anyone else. Not that March realized that.

Mom approached me, wrapping me in a tight embrace, "I feel like I haven't seen you in weeks. Are you feeling better?"

"Yes. I'm sorry I haven't come to see you." I felt guilty about how little time I dedicated to my mother, but life happened fast. Keeping Wonderland running was more time-consuming than I'd expected.

"Don't apologize. I have plenty of things to keep me busy. Just come see me sometime when it isn't for a big meeting." She said.

Caterpillar and Rab hugged quickly, before turning to us, "Don't let her lie to you. Anytime I come over to see her, she's running me off."

"You're always coming to my door with problems, Jonah." Mom shot back.

They continued to bicker, but I was distracted by Dina and Griffin's arrival. We'd offered to let them ride with us, but Dina had insisted she wanted Elsie to see the snow. "Give me my goddaughter," I said, taking Elsie immediately. She cooed at me before grabbing some of my hair and giving it a tug. "You're going to be big and strong just like your mama."

"Hey, now. I'm big and strong." Griffin said, "At least she has my eyes." He was right, of course; she had his hazel eyes. She still hadn't grown much hair, so it was hard to tell who she was going to take after in that regard. Otherwise, she could have been Dina's twin. Her facial features and skin tone were identical to her mother's.

"In any case, she's perfect," Dina said, pressing a kiss to Elsie's head. "How are you feeling, Ali? Cheshire told me what happened."

I rolled my eyes, "I'm fine. You know how dramatic they are."

"Griffin could stand to be a little more dramatic." She said, cutting her eyes to him.

"I can't live up to the standards of four different men. If you want that, you'd better start building your own harem." He said, before stuffing a piece of bread in his mouth.

We laughed, and Dina snorted, "I couldn't put up with four men the way you do."

Tillie, Cahir, and Jackson appeared in the doorway. I waved to them before handing Elsie back to Dina. "Tillie, I'm so glad you could come."

"Thanks for having us." She said, wrapping an arm around me for a moment, "You didn't have to include us in your family gathering."

"But then how would I give you your presents?" I joked, before I added, "Plus, at this point you are family."

"Well, this is far more relaxed than Lacie's Christmas. You know she just announced another pregnancy." Tillie muttered.

"Seriously? What is this number four? Is she planning to have one baby for every man she has?" I was shocked. Lacie and I weren't necessarily close, but I wouldn't have expected her to have another child after what happened at my wedding. Wonderland wasn't safe for anyone, much less children.

Tillie shrugged, "She said she has faith in the city's leadership. Plus, you know Victor would come unhinged if there was even a thought of harming Lacie or their kids. He hasn't been letting her out of the house hardly since…" She trailed off, realizing she was going to bring up my failed wedding.

"To each their own. Come, get comfortable." I said, waving them toward the large table that had been erected for everyone.

Sammy and Patrick arrived next, beelining to talk to Hatter. I watched as everyone I loved chatted and caught up casually. It wasn't often that we all got together when there wasn't a crisis to be handled. Waiters started to move in and out of the room, setting down steaming plates of food. I glanced at the clock. Duchess hadn't arrived. While she had only given a vague answer of whether she'd come or not, I'd really hoped she would. No one needed to be alone at Christmas time.

I took a seat between Hatter and Mom, dipping food out for myself. When I glanced up, Duchess was standing in the doorway. The bright red dress she wore hugged her body like a glove. I stood, slowly making my way over to her. "I'm glad you came."

She looked at me for a long moment, "Well, there's food and presents, how could I say no?"

I snorted, "Come take a seat." I pulled out the chair on the other side of Hatter. They had an interesting relationship now. They weren't exactly friends yet, but they had a history, so Hatter cared for Duchess in a strange way. It didn't bother me anymore. I knew Hatter wasn't going to leave me. His feelings about Duchess were purely platonic.

Once I was seated again, the voices rose as everyone got their food and began to eat. Dinner continued without a hitch, the food was delicious, and everyone slowly warmed up. Tillie and Duchess chatted about some event they'd both gone to recently. Lily and Cheshire's banter had my mother snorting wine out of her nose. Slowly, any anxiety fled from my body; my family was here and safe. We all got along even when it was hard.

"It's time for gifts," Rab announced as we all finished eating.

I jumped up, rushing to beat him to the gifts that had piled up in the corner. I grabbed a few packages and handed them off to Mom, Rab, and Lily, "March and I made these for you all. I won't say they're perfect, but you needed to fit in with the rest of us."

They all ripped into the carefully wrapped boxes. Mom gasped as she pulled out a pale green sweater. "It's beautiful."

March had agreed to teach me how to crochet so that we could make everyone sweaters. I'd done the ones for Mom, Lily, and Rab. I watched as March handed a package to Duchess. She opened it hesitantly, but I saw a slight mist in her eyes as she pulled the pink sweater out of the box, "It's definitely my color." She said, "Might be hard to style, but if anyone can do it, I can."

I smiled at her comments. She didn't know how to be part of our family yet, but one day she would. After everyone had opened their sweaters, we moved on to the other gifts. Lewis was entranced by a train set that Cheshire had apparently found. Elsie chewed on the ear of the rabbit that Lily had gotten for her.

Caterpillar's loud laugh caused me to turn toward him. Cheshire was holding a light blue bra like it was a snake.

"That would never fit you." I said, "Who is it from?"

"Me," Lily smirked. I couldn't stop myself from laughing as Cheshire threw the bra at him. "It will fit you." She muttered, tucking the fabric into my hand. "I thought that seemed like a good enough gift for the Cat."

Slowly, everyone finished unwrapping their gifts. I watched as Hatter went behind everyone and cleaned up the trash. I noticed his wrapped gifts set to the side, so I walked over, snatching the bag from his hands, "Go open your presents."

"It's okay, sweetheart. Someone needs to clean up." He argued, trying to take the bag back.

I turned my body away, keeping him from taking it from me, "Hayden O'Hare, get over there and open your presents right now."

He sighed, "Fine. I just don't like getting gifts."

"You'd better get used to it tonight. None of us have exchanged presents yet." I pointed out.

He sat down, slowly opening the first package. A brand new pair of sneakers that were a perfect dark green color was his first gift. I knew immediately that Ilaria had gotten them for him. She had accompanied him on several of his runs recently; she must have noticed he needed new shoes. He rushed through the rest of the packages, stopping to appreciate the dark orange sweater that March had made for him.

"Before we wrap up for the evening," Mom's voice floated over to us, "I just wanted to thank everyone for coming. The gifts were all lovely, but it's your company I appreciate the most. We have had a rough year, but I know that together we can deal with anything that comes our way."

We all shouted our agreements. This had been the best night we'd had as a family since we'd defeated the Red Queen. It gave me hope for our future. The Queen of Hearts couldn't take away the love we had for each other. We would fight for our happiness every day until the end of time if we had these moments together to look forward to.

Chapter 6

Cheshire

December 22nd, 2158

It was three days until Christmas, and I had no idea what to get Alice. I stared at her grainy image on the screen before me. Her fighting form was perfect as always, but the smile on her face as she ducked under a hit from Lily had me sitting down to watch. I knew it was wrong to keep an eye on her like this, but it let me know she was safe when she wasn't with me. If I could install a camera in every nook and cranny of Wonderland, I would. Especially if it would let me always have an eye on my woman. Alice was independent enough to make all of us neurotic about her safety. I'd been looking into ways to track her for months, but nothing I'd found was subtle enough for her not to know. The technology Wonderland had was nothing like it had been before the world ended. I didn't know how I could expand what we had access to, but it was one of the things I was working on.

"Did you find something for her yet?" Caterpillar's voice caused me to tilt back in my chair too far. Suddenly, I was lying on the floor staring at his black boots.

"No, I haven't," I muttered, standing up and returning my chair to the upright position.

"You'd better hope she never finds out about how much you watch her." He said, smirking. "She'd kick your ass."

"You won't tell her, because if you tell her that. I will tell her about what actually happened to her old leather jacket." I shot back.

"You wouldn't," Caterpillar growled.

I raised an eyebrow at him, "You want to bet?"

He shook his head, "That isn't why I came in here anyway. I've got a bad gut feeling. Have you seen anything else on the cams?"

"I haven't seen anything out of the ordinary. Have you checked in with Hatter or Sammy about the stakeout of Dodo's?" I asked.

"Yes, they haven't seen anything that would let us make a move on him..." He trailed off, lost in thought.

"Even villains have to take a break for Christmas, right?" I joked, trying to ease the tension in his shoulders.

He grunted before changing the subject, "Go get Alice something for Christmas. It's important to her. Keep an eye out for anything suspicious while you're out."

With that command, Caterpillar left the room, leaving me alone again. I turned my eyes back to Alice. She and Lily now lay on the gym floor, doing some kind of stretching I didn't know the name for. I turned off the monitor and spun around in the chair. I needed to go shopping.

I hated the snow. It was too cold, and as I took my second fall onto the ground, I cursed the Creator. I'd had no luck at the four stores that I'd gone to so far. I stared up into the sky, groaning at the feeling of the snow soaking into my clothes.

"Need a hand?" A familiar voice asked.

I stood up, coming eye to eye with Jackson and Cahir. "Just needed to take a break for a minute." I brushed off the snow from my jacket. "What are you both doing away from the mouse?"

"Christmas shopping," Cahir grumbled.

"Same here. Any luck?" I asked.

"Not a bit," Jackson responded, "What do you buy for a woman who wants nothing?"

"Don't ask me. I'm in the same boat as you. I've got no idea what to get Alice." I said, trudging toward the next store.

I was surprised that they both followed me and continued chatting. We'd never been particularly close. After all, Tillie and I had a tumultuous relationship, and she'd met them right after we broke up. It's not that Jackson or Cahir had ever been rude to me, but we also didn't casually talk. Until today.

"Here might be a good option," Cahir said, pointing toward a small store I hadn't noticed. There was no sign telling us the store's name, but the blue and pink dresses in the window gave me a decent idea of what they carried.

"Worth a try." I shrugged, following behind them.

The store wasn't well-lit, but I immediately knew Alice would love it. Clothes of every fabric and color lined the walls, and displays with various necklaces and other jewelry were strewn around the room. As we made our way to the back of the store, an older woman sat at the counter, seemingly asleep. Instead of bothering her, we continued to browse in silence. I noticed Jackson and Cahir both pick up several frilly intimate items that I had no doubt Tillie would adore. I was just about to give up when something caught my eye. I picked up the necklace, marveling at the dagger pendant. It was made of glass and looked as if flowers had been pressed into it. It screamed Alice.

"Only a special woman would like that necklace." A woman's voice spoke as I continued to inspect the piece.

"You're right. I think Alice would adore it. I'll take it." I said, gently resting the piece in the woman's outstretched palm.

"Young love is a beautiful thing; hold onto it tightly. Don't let the demands of life pull you away from one another." She advised as she placed the piece into a box, wrapping it carefully in red paper. "Thank you for shopping with me. Please come again."

"Thank you." I smiled as I waved at her, "Catch you guys another time." I shouted to Jackson and Cahir as I left. They were both laden down with items; I could see why Tillie had chosen them for herself. The three of them fit well together, just like the guys and I fit well with Alice.

I lurked into the apartment, hopeful that Alice was preoccupied with something else as I carried the small, wrapped package toward my office.

"What are you doing, cat?" Alice's voice startled me, and without thinking, I hid the box behind my back.

"You know this is the third time today someone has snuck up on me. I must be losing my touch." I joked, hoping to distract her as I inched toward my office.

"What are you hiding behind your back?" She responded, ignoring my distraction.

I sighed, "It's your Christmas gift. I'm going to go hide it now, where you will not find it until Christmas morning."

She grinned, following me toward my room without hesitation. I let her, carefully tucking the box under my arm so she wouldn't see it. If she did, she'd know I bought her jewelry immediately, and I wanted it to be a surprise. "Close your eyes and turn toward the door," I commanded her as we entered my room.

Her eyebrows shot up, "Are we going to get kinky, Ches?"

The heat in her eyes went straight to my dick. "Do as you're told."

She grinned, but turned around. I stared at her ass for a long moment, taking in the way the jeans she wore hugged it perfectly. I shook my head, opening one of my desk drawers and carefully placing the present inside.

I couldn't stop myself from grabbing a small toy that had been sitting there unused for several months. As I approached Alice, my nerves settled. I loved this woman; she was everything I had ever wanted. Today, we would try something new. I ran a hand down her back, gripping her ass through her jeans, "Strip and then go bend over my desk. Today we're going to do something new."

She stripped slowly, teasing me as each inch of her skin was revealed. She sauntered to the desk, presenting her perfect ass to me without a moment of hesitation. I nearly groaned from the sight of her body lit up by my computer screens. It was like one of my fantasies come to life. I caressed her gently, pressing kisses down her spine. When I came to her ass, I rubbed my thumb over her hole, causing her to tense. "It's okay, Ali. Don't you want to be able to take three of us at once?"

She moaned in response, and I moved my hand lower, slipping a finger into her wetness. "You're so turned on. Do you like the idea of me taking your ass?"

"Yes." She admitted.

"We're just going to start with a toy today, love. Are you ready?" I responded.

She nodded her consent, and that was all I needed. I grabbed the lube from a drawer to her left and squirted a generous amount on the butt plug. Slowly, I pressed it into her, bending down so I could gently tease her clit with my tongue as I pressed the toy into her ass. "Look at you, taking all of it so easily. I bet you could take my cock as well."

She groaned, "Please, Ches. I want you inside me. Let me cum on your cock."

I was rock hard, nearly about to finish in my pants at her words. As soon as the toy was settled inside of her, I stood, pushing my pants to my ankles and aligning myself with her entrance. I pushed in gently, allowing her to get used to the feeling of being full. She didn't wait for long before she was pushing back, fucking me as hard as I would allow her to. A tear ran down my face as I held off my orgasm. Being inside this woman was the closest to paradise that I'd ever find in this lifetime. "I'm going to cum, Al. You have to cum first."

"Yes, sir." She moaned, and I knew she was playing with herself. When her walls tightened and she shouted, I followed her into bliss, pumping my cum deep inside her. I was panting as I carefully directed us backward, collapsing into my desk chair with her in my arms.

"Did you enjoy that?" I finally asked.

She nodded, "It was a good distraction from the present."

I slapped her ass, "You are so bad."

"That's part of why you love me." Alice shot back.

"You're absolutely right," I said. We cuddled for a long time before she finally stood, excusing herself to shower before some meeting she had to attend.

When I was alone again, I stared at my screens. Alice truly changed my life so much in the time that I'd known her. I'd become so much closer to Hatter, March, and Caterpillar. They were more like brothers to me now than they had been before. We worked like a team with her as the leader. Caterpillar may never be able to admit it, but Alice was our leader, and she was damned good at it.

Chapter 7

Caterpillar

December 24th, 2025

There was nothing like the feeling of riding a motorcycle. It was even better when I had my woman's hot body pressed against my back as we flew through the streets of our city. It was our city after all. Everything we'd sacrificed to keep Wonderland safe made it ours. I hadn't originally planned to risk riding the bike in the snow, but when Alice woke up on Christmas Eve and begged to go out for a ride, I couldn't resist. The magick users had done a good job of clearing the roads, so it was clear enough to safely ride within the city limits.

I pulled off to the side, yanking my helmet off, "Are you about ready to turn around and head home?"

"I guess we can." There was a slight pout on her lower lip as I turned to face her more fully.

"The others would probably be up by now." I pointed out, "Maybe we could make cookies today. Pretend like we're all kids again."

Her face lit up at my words, "I'd love to do that."

"Then put your helmet back on and let's go," I commanded. I saw her roll her eyes, but she did pull the helmet back over her head. Before she could stop me, I gripped the chin of it, tightening the straps myself before doing the same to my own.

As we rode back through the city, I noticed smoke coming from a building nearby. Without a thought I turned the bike toward it. I heard Alice gasp as we turned onto the same road; one of the apartment buildings had flames licking up toward the sky. I'd barely parked the bike before she was jumping off, abandoning her helmet and running into the crowd of people.

I pulled my phone out, "Hatter, get in contact with Alcinda, have her call some magick users with water powers. We've got a building up in flames in sector three. Then get down here, we're going to need as many hands as possible." I hung up as soon as he confirmed that he understood my instructions.

I pushed through the crowd searching for Alice. To my horror, she came rushing out of the building with a small body under each of her arms. A woman came running up to her, tears streaming down her face. She handed the kids off to their mother before turning to rush back inside. I grabbed her arm, "Stop, you need to wait until we have more help. You're not fire resistant."

She growled, "Let me go. There are still people trapped inside." Before I could say anything else, she had slipped away. I ran after her, coughing as smoke rushed into my lungs. It hung heavy in the hallways, but Alice didn't react at all. She took the stairs, directing the people we ran into back down them as she passed. The further we traveled, the hotter it became and the thicker the smoke hung in the air. She stopped in front of a door and kicked it open. Three people lay passed out on the living room floor, fire crawling toward them. Alice didn't hesitate to grab the smallest of them, dragging the body from the room. I grabbed the other two, throwing them over each of my shoulders, and rushed out of the room, fire chasing me. We carried them back down the stairs as fast as we could without harming anyone. By the time we made it outside, my eyes burned and my muscles ached from carrying the two grown adults. I sat them down gently, allowing a man with a medical bag to check over them.

This time, when I grabbed Alice, she stopped, "You're too weak to carry an adult man down those stairs. Let me gather some men, and we will get everyone out that we can. The building isn't going to stay standing forever. Wait for the magick users to get here, coordinate their efforts to try to put out the flames."

She took a deep breath and nodded. I took a deep breath before grabbing a few men who stood at the entrance and directing them inside. We each took a floor, slowly getting everyone out of the building that we could find. Just as I sat down, the seventh person, Alice, came rushing up to me. "The building is going to collapse. No one else needs to go in."

"How do you know?" I asked, barely able to catch my breath.

"Mom had a vision. Told me to keep everyone out here until the magick users arrive." The pained look on her face had me pulling her into my arms.

"We saved twenty people, princess. We've done everything we could." I said.

"I know." Tears streaked down her face, leaving trails in the grey dust that coated her.

Just as I was about to respond, my phone rang, "Caterpillar."

"Get to Dodo's now." Cheshire's voice came through the phone.

"I can't-"

"The Queen of Hearts is there." He stopped me from responding.

Alice's eyes widened as she heard his words. We both turned, rushing toward the bike. "You don't think..." She trailed off, her blue eyes wide in horror at the thought we were both sharing. It was awfully convenient timing for a building to catch fire right as the Queen of Hearts is in the city, just a few blocks away.

"We'll find out," I growled, revving the bike as we flew away from the burning building.

We made it to Dodo's in record time, but I knew the moment we walked in the door we were too late. Dodo smirked at us, "What can I help the leaders of Wonderland with today?"

Alice grabbed his shirt, pulling him in close, "Where is that bitch?"

"Let me go! I don't know what you want, but you can't just go around accosting citizens." He shouted.

"That's where you'd be wrong. As the leaders of the city, we are within our rights to question anyone suspected of dealing with the Queen of Hearts." I said.

A bead of sweat dropped down his forehead. "You have no proof of that."

"Wrong." Alice smirked, "I have photos of the two of you together. That's enough for us to shut down your shop."

"No." Dodo gasped, "You can't."

"Wrong again," I said, "We can, and we are. As of today, you are officially closed. If we catch you selling a single weapon in Wonderland, I'll have you put in prison for the rest of your miserable life."

Alice released him, turning on her heel and walking toward the door, "We could have coexisted in peace, Dodo. Don't blame us for your bad decisions."

I nodded and followed her out of the shop without another word. "Let's go back to the building and make sure everyone is okay," I suggested.

Alice nodded, climbing on the back of the bike without another word.

We spent hours helping the people who had lived in the building that burned down. The magick users had managed to get the flames put out. There were still three people unaccounted for, but we had managed to save a total of twenty-seven people's lives. I still counted that as a win, but I could tell Alice had taken the deaths hard.

I scrubbed my face clean, letting the water wash away the ash and sweat that I was coated in. This was not how I had imagined the day going, but I needed to try to save it for Alice. She deserved to enjoy her favorite holiday. The Queen of Hearts' antics weren't going to change that. With that goal in mind, I finished my shower and dressed.

I walked into the living room where Alice was curled up with March, drinking a hot cup of tea. Her hair was still wet from where she'd showered, but March didn't seem to care as he braided her hair.

"Are you ready to make some cookies?" I asked, trying to seem as chipper as possible.

"We don't have to..." Alice trailed off.

"C-can you make lemon cookies?" March asked.

Alice nodded, but didn't move. I sighed, "Princess, what happened today isn't your fault. Without your help, more people would have died. Let's make some cookies, maybe we can make enough to pass out to the people who lost their homes."

She perked up at that idea, "I might need more ingredients."

"I'll go get anything you need." Cheshire said, "As long as I get at least three chocolate chip cookies."

A small smile graced Alice's face, "I think I can do that. Let me make a list."

I took a deep breath as she jumped up from the couch and rushed toward the kitchen.

"That was a good idea," Hatter said, patting my shoulder as he passed by. I watched as he bent down, pressing a kiss into March's hair. "She's been practically catatonic since she got home."

"How are we going to take down the Queen of Hearts when we can't even catch her for five minutes?" Cheshire growled.

"I don't know," I admitted. I had no idea what to do about her. Every time we got close to busting her, she managed to escape us. "I think she's taunting us."

"Probably." Hatter said, "We can deal with this problem after the holiday. Alice needs Christmas to go well."

"Agreed," I said, just as Alice reappeared from the kitchen.

"Here's everything I'm going to need to make all of the cookies. I'm going to get started on the first batch. Who is helping?"

"I think I'll j-just watch," March said.

"I'll help you, sweetheart." Hatter offered, making his way over to where she stood.

"You couldn't keep me out of the kitchen," I said.

"We'll see if you still feel that way when we're done making five hundred cookies," Alice said.

I would do anything if it meant that smile would stay on her face.

I never knew that baking was so messy. I had flour in places where flour should never be. As I pulled out the last batch of cookies from the oven, a shout nearly made me drop the pan. "What's wrong?" I shouted.

"Cheshire just scared me," Alice said, laughing as she came back into the kitchen. Her forehead was smeared with some red dye she'd added to some cookies. Her clothes were coated in a fine layer of flour and sugar, but she'd never looked more beautiful to me. "How did the last batch of lemon cookies turn out?"

I glanced down at the pan, "They look perfect to me, just like every other batch we've made."

"Well, why don't you leave those on the counter to cool. We should shower and get to bed. We'll hand out cookies after we open presents in the morning." She said.

"Maybe we should look at opening up a bakery sometime in the future. We're not going to run Wonderland forever." I said aloud. I'd been thinking about it for hours. Alice was so relaxed and happy as she baked and taught us how to make cookies. I could see her running a small bakery in the city when she was older.

She looked at me for a long moment before she finally said, "A bakery is a pipe dream, Roman. I may love to bake, but my passion is still our family. Our family will never be safe if I give up now."

"You put too much on your shoulders," I growled.

"Maybe that's why we're so well-suited. We both know the burden of leadership." She responded, "You can't honestly tell me you'd be happy just baking for the rest of your life. Leading Wonderland may not always be fun, but it does matter to you... to me."

Alice was so wise that sometimes I forgot that she was ten years younger than me. "That may be true, but your dreams still matter."

"I am living my dreams. I have you, Hatter, March, and Cheshire. My mother is still alive. Lily and Dina are safe and happy. There's nothing more I could ask for." She said.

My heart skipped a beat at her words, "I didn't know when I first met you that you were my dream, but you are."

She smiled, moving closer to me, "Your favorite pain in the ass." She breathed before reaching up to kiss me. I reached down, picking her up and setting her on the counter. "I love you."

"I love you too, princess." I glanced down at my watch, noticing the time, "Merry Christmas."

"Merry Christmas." She said, joy lighting up her blue eyes.

Chapter 8

❧❧❧ ❧❧❧

Alice

December 25th, 2158

All the guys had gotten up at seven this morning so that we could give cookies out before we went about the rest of our day. Watching the faces of the children light up as we handed out cookies on Christmas morning was enough to make up for the lack of sleep we'd gotten. Watching as they played in the snow outside the building we'd moved everyone into warmed my heart. The Queen of Hearts may have tried to ruin my holiday, but she had failed.

"Do you want to grab some breakfast before we head home?" Hatter asked.

"Pancakes?" Cheshire asked, appearing from nowhere.

"Waffles would be better." I argued, "Sure, but is anywhere actually open this morning?"

"That bistro we went to is." March piped in.

"That's not too far from here, let's walk," I said.

We waved goodbye to the families that still milled around outside and began our trek to the bistro. Everyone chatted as we walked, the sun finally making an appearance after two weeks of snow. It wasn't warm enough to melt any of the snow that was still on the ground, but I enjoyed the warmth on my face. As we turned the block, I felt a cold lump smack me in the face. I turned to find Cheshire giggling as he rushed to stand behind Caterpillar.

"Oh, it's on," I said, grabbing some snow in my hand and tossing it right at Caterpillar. He dodged, and the ball hit Cheshire square in the chest. Before I could celebrate, two snowballs hit me in the chest. Hatter and March both were belly laughing when I turned to glare at them. I grabbed Caterpillar, using him as a human shield as I gathered snow. I managed to nail Hatter right in the face as he tried to duck behind March. Cheshire snuck up and shoved snow down the back of my shirt, causing me to shriek. As we continued to play, other people joined in. Teams were made, and snowballs flew all over. It was the most relaxed I'd seen the people of Wonderland in my entire life.

I joined Caterpillar on the sidelines, panting from running around. "Having fun?" He asked.

"Most definitely, but I think I am ready for breakfast," I admitted.

"Better gather up those three menaces." He said, motioning to where Cheshire, Hatter, and March had built themselves a barricade out of snow. Kids pelted it with snowballs, every once in a while, Cheshire's purple and pink head would pop out and launch snowballs over the side.

Eventually, I was able to get their attention. They let the kids who had been attacking them take over their well-made barrier and jogged to join us. "Let's go get some food."

The bistro was quiet as we entered, with only a couple of people spread out across the room. We ordered enough food to fund the place for two weeks and found a booth in the corner to sit at. Thankfully, our food took no time to come out, and several plates of pancakes were passed out. A perfect plate of chocolate chip waffles had my mouth watering as the waitress set it down in front of me.

"Thank you." Caterpillar said, slipping some money into her hand once we had all of our food, "Merry Christmas."

Her eyes widened at the bills in her hand, "Merry Christmas... And thank you. Wonderland is a much safer place to live since you all... took over." She seemed unsure what else to say, so she rushed away before we could respond.

"We really don't hear that enough," Cheshire muttered, before he began stuffing pancakes in his mouth.

"We can't expect most people to notice the difference." Hatter said, "The changes have primarily affected the upper-class citizens and the magick users."

"How can we change the everyday people's lives?" I asked.

"We are. Everything we do affects every person in Wonderland. It just may seem small to them right now. They have more freedom and safety than they had last year. Change takes time." Caterpillar responded.

I decided to stuff my mouth full of the perfect waffles to avoid responding. I knew he was right, but it felt like most of the time we didn't get recognized for the work we had done. That was selfish, of course, I didn't do anything, I did for recognition. Eventually, things would change enough that everyone would be affected. I wouldn't stop until that was true.

We ate in a comfortable silence, enjoying the food and being together. It wasn't often we got to all spend time together without stress. Once we were done eating, we walked slowly back to the apartment building. The lights sparkling in the windows of each room brought a smile to my face. My family was safe and each of them were at home celebrating Christmas together.

"Someone should call Duchess and invite her over for lunch," Hatter said, as we all took our coats and shoes off in the entryway.

"Are you sure?" Cheshire asked, "She's... hard to get along with sometimes."

"I think it's a good idea. If she says no, we won't push, but she is my cousin." I responded.

Hatter was picking up the phone and making the call before anyone could argue. We all stood with bated breath as he had the fastest conversation I'd ever heard. When he stuck his phone back in his pocket, he cringed, "I think she'll come, but she was not happy that I woke her up."

"It's ten in the morning." Caterpillar pointed out.

"Not everyone lives on your early bird schedule." Cheshire said, "Now, is it time to open presents yet?"

I clapped my hands, "It's Christmas, and we haven't opened presents yet. We must remedy this immediately." I rushed toward the living room, grabbing an armful of presents as the guys took seats around the room. I handed each of them a gift before taking a seat on the floor and opening the box that had my name on it. I tore through the pretty red wrapping paper to reveal a beautiful wooden box engraved with flowers that reminded me of my wildflower field.

"That's from m-me. I thought you'd like it... if--"

Before March could continue, I flung myself into his arms. "It's perfect! I love it."

March opened his gift from Hatter next, a new medical kit with his name stitched on the outside. If I had to guess, Hatter did the stitching himself. It was slightly messy, but absolutely a perfect gift considering how often we all got hurt. Cheshire opened up his gift from Caterpillar next, a new gun cleaning kit. I snorted. The guys always bought each other practical things, but at least they seemed happy with it. I opened my gift from Hatter next, a brand new brown leather jacket had my eyes welling with tears. My last one had disappeared, and while it was ratty and disgusting, it had been my favorite item to wear.

"Don't cry. Please don't cry." Hatter begged.

I sniffed, "I'm not. I'm not. Thank you, Hayden. It's exactly what I wanted."

Caterpillar opened his gift from March, and I went from nearly crying to hysterically laughing in moments. March had made black crocheted gloves, but also included a ridiculous-looking hat that turned out to be a crocheted helmet. "This would never protect someone in an accident."

I snorted, "No, but you couldn't say I'm not wearing a helmet."

Caterpillar glared at me, but didn't have a chance to respond as Cheshire shoved a small box into my hands. I recognized it as the package he'd tried so hard to hide from me just a few days before. I opened the wrapping carefully. As I opened the small velvet box, a gasp left my mouth. A perfect glass dagger necklace was filled with blue pressed flowers. I pulled it from the box, handing it to Cheshire carefully. Once he had it secured, it hung perfectly between my breasts. I wrapped my arms around him, "It's beautiful."

"Not as beautiful as you." He responded.

We continued to open presents until all the packages were opened. Caterpillar was shining his new boots, and Cheshire had disappeared into his office with some odd electronic box that Hatter had gotten for him. Hatter and March were playing with the glass chess set I'd bought for March. I smiled before disappearing into the kitchen to start lunch. I had decided to go all out for our Christmas lunch: Ham, various types of beans and vegetables, smashed potatoes, homemade bread, and an apple pie. It wasn't easy to get apples in Wonderland, but I'd managed to get just enough for us to have a pie for Christmas. I hummed as I worked, completely unaware of my surroundings as I cooked a meal for the loves of my life.

"Duchess is here," Cheshire hollered, catching my attention for the first time since I'd stepped into the kitchen. I finished placing the pie into the oven, and walked into to greet her. Duchess was wearing jeans and the pink sweater that March had made for her.

I smiled as I approached her, wrapping my arms around her. She patted my shoulder awkwardly, but I ignored it, "I'm glad you came."

"I brought some mead for everyone." She responded. "It smells good in here."

"We'll be ready to eat in about ten minutes. Cheshire, will you go set the table?" I asked.

He looked at me strangely for a moment. We had never used our large dining room table before. It was always easier to take our meals at the counter or in the living room. It wasn't as often as I'd like that we all sat down together, but today I was going to insist on it.

Everyone filed into the dining room slowly, chatting casually as Caterpillar, Duchess, and I carried out all of the food.

"Damn, Ali. This all looks amazing." Hatter said as he reached for a slice of ham.

Caterpillar smacked his hand, "The ladies get their plates first."

Duchess snorted as she grabbed a plate, piling it high with all of the food. I followed suit before taking my seat between Caterpillar and March. As we all ate, the conversation flowed easily, even Duchess seemed relaxed. The food turned out even better than I expected.

As we all sat around with full bellies and hearty laughter filling the room, a sense of true happiness filled me. Christmas had been perfect, even with all the trials leading up to this special day, it had turned out better than I could have hoped. My guys had ensured that I enjoyed the holiday that I loved so much. Duchess being here was the icing on the cake. I hoped that one day she and I would be as close as I was to Dina. I knew that would take time, but this was a great start.

As we moved into the living room, I glanced out the window, seeing that snow was once again falling over the streets of Wonderland. I'd never seen so much snow in my life; it felt like a sign. Today, I wasn't going to worry about our problems or the future. The only thing that truly mattered was the people who surrounded me. Love would persevere through it all.

Epilogue

Eumonia

Azura's wings flapped in my mind's eye as she took a seat on the ledge of the window. Through her eyes, I saw Alice, grinning as she sliced a piece of pie. My heart squeezed as she nearly fell, Roman catching her just before the plate would have hit the floor. Even through the bird's eyes, I could see the love that had bloomed between them. Azura sat there watching as the small group laughed and basked in each other's company.

When Vivica stood to leave, I gave Azura the signal to fly home. I didn't want to witness a private moment between the group of young people. Snow was falling heavily as she made her way back to me. I had considered roaming the streets today, enjoying the silence as the snow once again piled up. Ultimately, I'd decided against it. While I loved Wonderland, there was a bitterness to roaming the city. I could never again be part of the society that I loved so dearly.

Azura landed on my outstretched hand, shaking the snow from her feather before I made my way inside my modest home. I spoke aloud as I stoked the fire, "It's good Alice has such wonderful men in her life. She'll need them for what is to come." I glanced at the bird, who squawked in acknowledgement, "I agree, it may be an unusual arrangement to us, but the Creator never makes mistakes. Those men will play a large role in her journey." She cawed softly, nuzzling her head against my cheek. I had always loved animals more than people, but since the beginning of my isolation, the birds of Wonderland had been very special to me. Azura was the most human-like of them all. I often wondered if my magick had some effect on her. I hummed as I poured myself a bowl of porridge. I rarely made my way into town for meat and vegetables to feed myself. While I should have considered the holiday, this food would be just as filling. "Someday very soon, Azura, things are going to change. Don't feel sad for me today, little love. Tomorrow is the dawn of a new day."

I'd long wondered when the day would come that the visions that had haunted me through my long life would see fruition. I'd seen the beginning just over a year ago, when Alice displayed her powers for all of Wonderland to see. That moment, whether she knew it or not, was the beginning of a far-reaching journey. One that I hoped would end in a better future for all.

As I sat down at my small table, a piping hot bowl of food before me, I said a small prayer, "Creator, let my work have meant something. Let all that I have been through make a difference for her."

Before I began to eat, I ran a hand down the soft feather of Azura, "Merry Christmas, my friend. May next year fulfill all of our dreams."

Acknowledgements

The first thing I want to shoutout is the Kraken's Cup in Knoxville Tennessee. It is an adorable, English style tea shop owned by the amazing Vallie. Their support of my work has meant the world to me, and certainly inspired Alice and March's experience at the tea shoppe.

As always, my husband Tyler, deserves all the credit for putting up with my insanity. His support is the only reason all my books happen. And a huge thank you to my family, while I may not love the holiday season, I wouldn't want to spend it with anyone else.

A big shout to my ARC and street team. Without them my books would be a mess, and no one would know about them. I also have to shoutout, Leah, who once again did an amazing job on the cover.

And finally, to every person who reads Code White, thank you. Without you I wouldn't be an author at all.

About the author

Taila Cantrell can be found lurking in the mountains of East Tennessee with her husband. Whether she's at her day job, wrangling the feral blue-collar men, tucked into a local bookstore, or at home curled up with her many cats and two pups, she's always plotting the next story. Her readers can look forward to many genres from fantasy romance to poetry to murder mysteries there is no story Taila isn't willing to give her voice to.

In every story, Taila blends spellbinding romance with trauma, chaos, and hope. Her books remind readers that even in the darkest moments, the heart still remembers how to burn bright.

Also by

The Reclaiming Wonderland Series
Code Red
Code White: Frosted Wonderland
Blue Dreams
Emerald Knights (Coming April 2026)

The Austral Witches:
Primal Echoes
One Bloody Night
Two Shadowed Hearts
Three Little Doves (Coming February 2026)
Four Twisted Dreams (Coming March 2026)

Mercy Valley:
Wing of the Dragon (Coming May 2026)

The Tides of Desire Trilogy w/Allena Scott
A Tide of Secrets and Storms